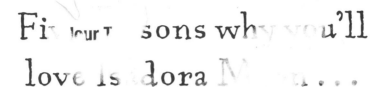

Find four reasons why you'll love Isadora Moon...

Meet the magical,
fang-tastic Isadora Moon!

Isado... bit,

All the fun of the
with added sparkle and bite.

Isadora's family is crazy!

Enchanting
pink and black
pictures

What do you love about the funfair?

The rides because they are fast and wicked!
– Zhakya

I love the pink sticky cotton candy!
– Libby

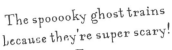
The spooooky ghost trains because they're super scary!
– Freya

I love trying to win giant teddies!
– Miss Jarman

I like hot dogs that are as big as your arm!
– Sienna

I love the candyfloss because it's so FLUFFY!
– Anna

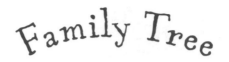

Family Tree

My Mum
Countess Cordelia
Moon

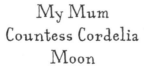

Baby Honeyblossom

My Dad
Count Bartholomew
Moon

Me!
Isadora Moon

Pink Rabbit

For vampires, fairies and humans everywhere!
And for Grandpa and Dulcie.

OXFORD
UNIVERSITY PRESS

Great Clarendon Street, Oxford OX2 6DP

Oxford University Press is a department of the University of Oxford.
It furthers the University's objective of excellence in research, scholarship, and
education by publishing worldwide. Oxford is a registered trade mark of Oxford
University Press in the UK and in certain other countries

First published 2018

British Library Cataloguing in Publication Data

Data available

ISBN: 978-0-19-276710-3

1 3 5 7 9 10 8 6 4 2

Printed in Great Britain by Bell and Bain Ltd, Glasgow

Paper used in the production of this book is a natural,
recyclable product made from wood grown in sustainable forests.
The manufacturing process conforms to the environmental
regulations of the country of origin.

```
        MIX
        Paper from
FSC   responsible sources
www.fsc.org  FSC® C007785
```

ISADORA · MOON

Goes to the Fair

Harriet Muncaster

OXFORD
UNIVERSITY PRESS

Chapter ONE

It was Saturday morning and the sun was shining through our windows. It made me feel all happy and sparkly, and as though something interesting might be about to happen.

'I wonder what it will be,' I said to Pink Rabbit as we made our way down the stairs to breakfast.

Pink Rabbit bounced up and down
beside me. He used to be my favourite
stuffed toy but my mum magicked him
alive with her wand. She can do things
like that because she's a fairy!
'Good morning Isadora,'
yawned Dad, who
was just

coming in through the front door. He had
been on his nightly fly. Dad is a vampire
so he stays up all night and sleeps during
the daytime. He stepped into the hallway
and I noticed that he was standing on
a colourful piece of paper lying by the
doormat.

'What's that? I said, pulling it out from under his shiny black shoe.

'Junk mail probably,' said Dad.

But it didn't look like junk mail to me. As I smoothed out the crumples, I saw that the piece of paper was a big, glittering poster with a picture of a carousel in the middle of it. The carousel was covered with fairy lights and spinning under a starry sky. Delighted children sat on top of fancily dressed ponies, holding clouds of pink fluffy candyfloss in their hands. FUNFAIR SPECTACULAR! shouted the twirly pink writing above the carousel. NEXT WEEKEND ONLY!

'Oh wow, Dad!' I said. 'Can we go? Please?'

'Hmm,' said Dad, as I followed him into the kitchen. 'I'm not sure. Ask Mum.'

Mum was at the kitchen table, spooning some strawberry yoghurt into my baby sister Honeyblossom's mouth.

I held the poster up for her to see.

'Look Mum!' I said. 'Can we go?'

'A fair?' said Mum dubiously. 'A human fair . . . I'm not sure. Ask Dad.'

'I've asked Dad!' I said exasperatedly. 'He told me to ask you!'

'Oh,' said Mum, taking another look at the poster. 'Well . . . '

'Please,' I begged.

'Wouldn't you rather go to a vampire fair?' asked Dad. 'I used to love going to vampire fairs with my friends, when I was a young boy. All those lovely spooky rides lit by flickering candles in the dead of night. And delicious red food. My favourite ride used to be the coffin blaster.'

'Or a fairy fair,' suggested Mum quickly. 'Fairy fairs are lovely. All full of flowers and beautiful nature. I used to like going on the little flower-cup ride with my friends.'

'Pfft!' said Dad. 'The coffin blaster is

much more exciting!'

'But not as pretty,' pointed out Mum.

'Oh but I really, *really* would like to go to the Funfair Spectacular,' I said. 'And it's only on next weekend. Please can we go? I promise I'll tidy my whole bedroom!'

'Maybe,' said Mum. 'We'll think about it.'

When I went to school the following week, I asked my friends if they had seen that the Funfair Spectacular had come to town.

'I saw a poster on my way to school!' said Zoe. 'I'm going to ask my mum if she'll take me!'

'I want to go too,' said Bruno. 'I'm going to ask my Dad.'

'So am I!' said Jasper.

My friends all started chattering excitedly about the fair.

'I want to go on the roller coaster,' said Sashi. 'I've heard it has one hundred loops!'

'One hundred!' gasped Bruno. 'I'm definitely going on that!'

'I'm not,' shuddered Samantha, looking fearful. 'I prefer the teacups.'

'Teacups are boring,' said Jasper. 'The dodgems and the ghost train are much more exciting!'

'Ooh yes, the ghost train!' said Zoe, shivering with glee. 'And we can eat candyfloss and hot dogs.'

'I love candyfloss!' cried Sashi. 'It's like eating clouds!'

'Will you come, Isadora?' said Zoe,
looking at me. 'I bet you've never been
to a human fair before.'

'I haven't,' I said. 'And I *really* want to
go. I'll have to ask Mum and Dad again.'

All day I thought about how I
would persuade them to let me go, and by
evening I had thought of a whole list of
things I could do.

'Mum,' I said. 'If you take me to the
fair I promise to water all your lovely fairy
plants for a whole week. And I'll help to
change Honeyblossom's nappies every
day. And feed her pink milk. AND I'll even
have all my baths in the garden pond from
now on, to be close to nature.'

Mum laughed.

'That's very kind Isadora,' she said,
'but—'

'And Dad,' I continued. 'I promise to
polish all your special vampire silver. And

hang my cape up properly by the front door, so that it doesn't get creased. I'll tidy my bedroom, and I *might* even brush my hair.'

'Wow,' said Dad, looking shocked. 'You must really want to go to the fair!'

'I do!' I said, thinking about the glittering carousel and the candyfloss and all the sparkling fairy lights. I wanted to spin round and round on one of those fancy-looking ponies, with my hair flying out in the breeze.

'Well,' said Mum. 'I *was* going to say that we had decided we would take you anyway. But as you've offered to do all these lovely things for us . . .'

'It would be rude of us not to accept!' finished Dad. 'My silverware is all laid out in the dining hall. I was thinking about polishing it this evening, but you can do it instead. There's only one hundred and ninety-nine pieces.'

'And I think Honeyblossom does need a change,' said Mum, sniffing the air. 'You can do that too!'

I stared in horror at my baby sister, who was sitting, gurgling, in her high chair. I had never changed a nappy before.

'Um . . .' I said, feeling my cheeks turn bright pink.

Mum and Dad both burst out laughing.

'It's alright, Isadora,' said Mum. 'We're only joking.'

'Though it would be nice if you tidied your room,' said Dad.

'Yes, that would be lovely,' agreed Mum. Then suddenly she frowned and slapped her hand to her forehead. 'Wait!' she said. 'I forgot! Your cousins are coming next weekend! We can't go to the fair. I'm sorry, Isadora, it had completely slipped my mind.'

'But couldn't we all go?' I suggested. 'I bet Mirabelle and Wilbur would enjoy the fair.'

'Well . . . I *suppose* we could ask them,' said Mum. 'And it would keep your naughty cousin Mirabelle out of mischief, at least.'

'Oh goody!' I said, hugging Pink Rabbit excitedly to my chest. 'I can't wait!'

Chapter TWO

On the morning of the fair I woke up
bright and early and jumped out of bed.
I was so excited.

'When will Mirabelle and Wilbur
be here?' I asked as I ate my breakfast.

'Not until late afternoon,' said
Mum, looking at the clock. 'In about
nine hours.'

'Nine hours?!' I said. 'That's ages!'

'I'm sure you'll find something to do,' said Mum. 'Why don't you tidy your bedroom, like you promised?'

'Okaaay,' I sighed.

It took me ages to tidy my room, because it was so boring. The hours crept by very slowly. I watched the clock as it tick-tocked towards lunch and then tick-tocked into the afternoon.

'How long now?' I asked, staring out of the kitchen window.

'About one hour,' said Mum, who was busy whipping up a strawberry cake. 'You can help me decorate the cake if you like.'

I stood by the table and sprinkled sugar bats and pink stars onto the swirly strawberry icing, but I kept one eye on the window. Eventually I saw a movement in the clouds outside.

'They're here!' I yelled, leaping towards the front door and opening it wide. Two figures were coming down through the clouds on broomsticks. My witch fairy cousin Mirabelle and her wizard fairy brother, Wilbur.

'Isadora!' shouted Mirabelle, landing on the ground and then running forward to hug me. She had obviously been spraying herself with her mum's witchy perfumes, because she smelled strongly of marzipan and purple berries.

'I'm so excited to go to the fair!' she said. 'Wilbur is too!'

'I suppose so,' said Wilbur, shrugging as though he was too important for the fair.

'We've never been to a human one before,' said Mirabelle. 'Mum's taken us to a witch one though. It was really fun. There was an amazing broomstick whirligig and a fortune-telling tent and a black-cauldron waltzer.'

'There was,' nodded Wilbur, starting to look a bit more excited. 'I liked the wizard-hat helter skelter best. It was a giant pointy wizard's hat with a slide twirling all the way down.'

'I hope there'll be some fun rides at this fair,' continued Mirabelle. 'I like the fast ones.'

We all went inside and had some tea and cake while we waited for Dad to wake up. Being a vampire, he sleeps through the day and wakes up in the evening. I got the poster of the Funfair Spectacular from my bedroom and showed it to Mirabelle and Wilbur.

'It *does* look exciting,' said Wilbur.
'Though it is missing the wizard-hat
helter skelter.'

'It still looks very pretty and magical
though,' said Mirabelle.

'It looks almost like the fairy fairs
I used to go to as a child,' said my mum.
'Me and your dad used to have such fun
at them together. Has your dad ever taken
you to a fairy fair?'

Wilbur and Mirabelle shook their
heads.

'Ahh,' said Mum. 'Get him to take you
one day. They are so lovely.' She started
to tell us about all the wonderful things
that went on at fairy fairs: the teacup

flowers, the cones of sugared violet sweets,
the little leaf boats in the boating pond.
She was still chattering away when Dad
appeared in the kitchen, yawning and
stretching.

'Good evening,'
he said. 'Hello
Mirabelle, hello
Wilbur!'

'Hello Uncle
Bartholomew,' they
said.

Once we had
finished our tea,
and Dad had drunk
his red juice, we

put on our shoes and got ready to go
out to the fair. It was a lovely warm
evening and I felt my insides fizz with
excitement as we walked down the road
towards the town. As we walked,

I reminded everyone that this was a
human fair.

'There won't be any magic,'
I said. 'And we mustn't do any magic
there either.'

'Absolutely,' said Mirabelle.

'Of course!' said Mum, waving her wand in the air. 'I understand!' Little stars sparkled in the sky for a minute and then disappeared. Mum stared at them happily.

'So pretty!' she breathed.

I pointed at the wand.

'That's the kind of thing I mean,' I said. 'You need to hide that in your bag.'

'Oh,' said Mum. 'Yes, of course.'

Hurriedly, she stowed the wand away in
her handbag.

'Good!' I said, running ahead of
everyone and rounding the corner.
I wanted to be the first to see the fair!
I had visions of twinkling fairy lights
and stripy tents and beautiful, colourful,
sparkling rides . . . but what I saw made
me stop in my tracks.

'Is this it?' asked Wilbur, sounding
disappointed.

'It looks a bit shabby to me,' remarked
Dad, pursing his lips.

'It's not very busy, is it?' said Mum.

FUNFAIR
SPECTACULAR

Chapter THREE

The Funfair Spectacular did not look very spectacular at all. In fact it looked particularly *un*spectacular. The stripy tents were grey and tattered, the rides sounded clanky and rattly, the music was so quiet you could barely hear it, and the fairy lights were fizzing and spluttering as though they were about to go out.

The people operating the rides looked sad and grey too. They had worry lines all over their faces.

'Oh dear . . .' said Mum sadly. 'What a shame.'

My heart suddenly felt very small and tight. I held on to Mum's hand for a minute because my eyes were feeling a bit prickly. Suddenly I wasn't sure if I wanted to visit a human fair after all. Perhaps I should have listened to Mum and Dad, and gone to a vampire or a fairy one. I felt embarrassed to have brought my whole family here.

'Maybe we should go home,' I suggested.

'Nonsense!' said Mum, who always liked to look on the bright side. 'We've only just got here! It's not that bad, Isadora. The rides are only a little bit run-down. Nothing a bit of magic can't fix.'

'Ooh yes!' said Mirabelle, rubbing her hands together gleefully. 'I bet we could make this human fair a whole lot more exciting!'

'No!' I cried worriedly. 'No magic, remember?'

FUNFAIR SPECTACULAR

'Okay,' said Mum, sounding
slightly disappointed. 'Well, let's go in
anyway. I fancy a ride on the teacups.'

'The teacups!' scoffed Mirabelle.
'I think we should go on the roller
coaster! Or the ghost train!'

I didn't feel like going on any
of the rides, but I followed my
family into the fair and towards
the roller coaster. As we got closer
I could see that the paint was faded
and peeling.

'At least we won't have to queue!'
said Dad cheerfully, as we walked up to
the man in the ticket booth.

'Tickets for five, please,' he said.

The man in the booth looked delighted.

'Five!' he exclaimed. 'Excellent! That's the most tickets we've sold so far tonight!'

'Why?' asked Dad. 'Are you not getting many customers?'

'Not as many as we used to,' admitted the man.

'What a shame,' said Mum.

'It is,' agreed the man. 'The problem is that a lot of our rides need updating but we haven't had enough customers lately to be able to afford to do it. And the customers don't come because the rides really do need a spruce up! A lick of paint! You can see the pickle we're in.'

'I can,' said Dad, nodding. 'It's a conundrum.'

'A conundrum?' said the man, scratching his head.

'It's a fancy word for a pickle,' Dad explained.

'Ah,' said the man. 'Yes, it really is a conundrum. I do hope we'll be able to think of a solution soon, or we might have to close the fair down. It would be such a shame. It's a family run business, you know. Started by my

great-grandfather. It's travelled all over
the country, and it's been going for almost
one hundred years!'

'Gosh!' exclaimed Mum. 'One
hundred years!'

'Well in that case,' said Dad kindly,
'we'll take two rides!' He put some
money down on the counter and we all
stepped into the roller-coaster carriages.
It was my first roller-coaster ride and
I felt a bit nervous. Pink Rabbit was
nevous too, he had his paws over his
eyes. A little bell trilled, and suddenly
the carriages lurched into life. They
went clanking and clunking up the track
and then stopped at the top.

'Hang on!' called the man from below.
'There's been an error!'

We saw him fiddling about with some buttons, and then suddenly the carriage whooshed over the top of the track and swooped downwards. It looped the loop and then came to another standstill, in the middle of the track.

'Well this is no good!' said Dad.

'It is a bit rubbish,' agreed Mirabelle.

'It's perfectly fast enough for me!' said Mum, who had her eyes tightly shut.

'Hmm,' said Mirabelle naughtily.
'I think this ride could use just a little
bit of help.' Before I could stop her,
she whipped out a little potion bottle
and sploshed the contents onto the
rollercoaster track. Immediately, the
peeling paint began to repair itself.
The dilapidated carriages became new
and shiny once again. The clanking and
clunking stopped, and suddenly we
were gliding smoothly along the track
at super high-speed. My hair blew out
behind me and my tummy felt like it
was turning upside down.

'Woohoo!' shrieked Mirabelle. 'This
is much more fun!'

After it had been round the track twice, the carriage came to a stop and we all tumbled out on wobbly legs.

'I don't know what happened!' the ticket booth operator was saying to another fair worker. 'The ride just suddenly transformed! Look at it. Good as new!'

I frowned at Mirabelle and reminded her that this was a human fair.

'Really, we shouldn't be using any magic,' I said.

'I know, I know!' said Mirabelle. 'But surely just a little bit won't matter.'

'Yes,' agreed mum. 'A teensy bit won't make much of a difference. I mean, honestly, that roller coaster was a health-and-safety hazard!'

'It was a bit,' agreed Dad. 'And look how pleased the ticket man is!'

I looked and saw that the man was beaming. He looked like he might burst with happiness.

'Maybe we *should* just do a little fixing here and there,' whispered Mum. 'You know, just to help them out a bit.'

'I think so,' said Dad.

'Me too!' said Mirabelle, excitedly.

'And me!' said Wilbur.

'Umm . . .' I began. I wasn't sure if it

was a good idea. Humans are not used to magic. It might scare the customers away, rather than bring them in.

'I vote for the teacups next,' said Mum. 'It's such a sophisticated ride.'

'Boring, more like,' whispered Wilbur, as we made our way over to them.

Dad bought our tickets and we split ourselves between four of the teacups. The fifth one was broken with a huge crack in one side of it. The ride started and we began to spin around slowly, creaking and juddering.

'Lovely,' said Mum.

'Booooring!' yawned Wilbur.

I saw him wave his hands about in a wizardy sort of way. Little sparks erupted from his fingers.

'What are you doing?' I whispered.

'Just helping it along a bit,' said Wilbur. Suddenly we began to spin so fast that everything became a blur and I began to feel a bit sick.

'Wilbur!' shouted Dad. 'Undo that spell this instant!!'

'This isn't what we meant by fixing the rides!' said Mum, as her flower crown blew off her head.

Through the blur I saw Wilbur's hands working to try and undo the spell he had cast. Eventually the teacups

slowed down and resumed their juddering and creaking. Now I could focus properly, I could see the ride operator standing there with his mouth open. He was blinking his eyes and shaking his head in confusion.

'Let me do it,' said Mum, taking out her wand and giving it a little wave, so that glitter fell all around us. At once, the juddering and creaking stopped and we began to spin round as though everything was perfectly oiled. The crack in the broken teacup mended itself instantly.

'That's better,' she said. 'I might just add one more little improvement.'

'No!' I cried. 'We've done enough!'

But mum had already waved her
wand and suddenly instead of teacups,
we were sitting in giant, living, perfumed
flowers that spun around gently and
played beautiful tinkly music.

'Much more nature friendly,' smiled Mum happily.

The new 'teacups' were lovely and the ride operator looked delighted, but I still felt nervous about using magic at a human fair.

'Stop worrying, Isadora!' said Wilbur. 'Just relax!'

But I noticed that his nose had turned very red.

'Atishoo!' he said. 'ATISHOO!'

'Oh help!' shrieked Dad suddenly, leaping out of his flower. 'Bees are coming!' He covered himself in his cape and crouched down on the ground.

'Bees won't harm you!' sang Mum as she watched more and more of them buzz towards the flowers. 'They're a very important part of nature!'

But Mirabelle, Wilbur, and I all jumped out of our flower cups too and stood on the grass, away from the big flowers and the bees.

'Atishoo,' said Wilbur again. 'I think that ride has sparked off my hayfever.'

'Mum!' I called. 'You need to undo your spell!'

'But why?' said Mum. 'The flowers are so beautiful! Look at them!'

'The bees,' whimpered Dad from under his cape. 'The bees . . .'

Mum rolled her eyes and waved her wand. The flower cups turned back into ordinary

teacups, but now they looked fresh and
brand new. I breathed a sigh of relief and
Dad peeped out from under his cape.

'Can we stop doing magic now?'
I asked, as we all walked away from the
ride.

'Yes of course,' said Dad distractedly.
'Ooh look, the dodgems!'

'My favourite!'
said Wilbur.

'Mine
too!' said
Mirabelle,
grabbing a
rusty car and
hopping into it.

She began to race around, shrieking with laughter every time she managed to bash into Wilbur.

'Hey Mirabelle!' shouted Wilbur. 'Calm down!'

'Yes, be careful!' said Dad, who was driving carefully round the edge of the floor, making sure to give way and stay on the left.

'This is fun!' said Mirabelle as she zoomed her car towards Wilbur and bumped into him, so that his wizard's hat fell over his eyes.

'So fun!' said Wilbur, doing a U turn and bumping right back into her. 'Got you, Mirabelle!'

'Got you both!' laughed Mum, who was sitting next to me and holding the wheel. She whizzed past them, crashing into both their cars and then made a beeline for Dad, who was gliding about elegantly, avoiding everyone so that no one bashed into him and messed up his hair. She gave him a little bump to the back of his dodgem.

'What fun!' she whooped.

'You know what would make it more fun?' said Dad, as he smoothed his hair back down into its perfectly perfect quiff. 'These dodgems would be much improved if they had bat wings and could fly in the air.'

'Oh no!' I said. 'You said no more magic. Let's leave them as they are!'

'But bat wings would be amazing!' said Dad. 'Vampire-bat cars! Oh come on, just one more little spell!'

'Let's do it!' shouted Mirabelle, as she screeched past us. I saw her let go of the wheel and get out her potion kit once again. She mixed something up at

lightning speed and threw it into the air.
The dodgems transformed into sleek,
black, bat-winged cars and began to
rise upwards.

'Wheeee!' shouted Mirabelle, as she sailed around after Wilbur. 'I'm coming to get you!'

'Not if I get you first!' shouted Wilbur.

By the time we had finished our ride on the dodgems, a little crowd had gathered by the edge of the ride. Not just funfair workers but passers by too. They were all staring at the dodgems in amazement. I spotted some of my school friends in the crowd and waved.

'I want a go on these!' I heard Bruno say.

'See,' said Mum, patting my arm as we walked by. 'A little bit of magic is not

a bad thing. See how
many customers are
starting to come!'

'I suppose so,' I said,
starting to feel a little less worried.
'Can we get some candyfloss now?'

Chapter FOUR

We made our way to the food stall,
which smelled of hot dogs and burnt
sugar. Mum got us a stick of candyfloss
each. It tasted like clouds!

'Yum,' I said, biting into the fluff,
which melted immediately on my
tongue.

'You know what would make this

candyfloss really exciting?' said Mum,
waving her wand before anyone could
say anything. 'If it changed flavour with
every bite!'

Sparkles rained down on us, and
the next time I bit into my candyfloss
I tasted cherry pie.

'Ooh, butterscotch!' said Mirabelle.

'Chocolate cake!' said Wilbur.

'Frogspawn,' said Dad wrinkling
his nose.

'Oh,' said Mum, 'hang on.' She
waved her wand again.

'Red juice!' said Dad. 'My favourite!'

I stared up at the sky, which was
beginning to darken, and at the fairy
lights that were fizzing and spluttering all

over the fairground. Some of the
bulbs were broken. After all the magic
we had already done, fixing the fairy
lights wouldn't make much of a difference.
Why shouldn't I help out
a little bit too?

'Can I try and mend them?' I asked.

'Good idea,' said Dad.

I closed my eyes tight and waved
my wand above me, shooting a shower
of sparks into the air. The broken lights
began to twinkle and glow, and the fizzing
and spluttering stopped.

'Lovely, Isadora,' said Mum.

Then I had another irresistible idea.
I waved my wand again, and this time the
lights changed shape. Now they were all
star and moon and bat shaped.

'Ooh, pretty!' said Mirabelle.

I felt my face glow pink with pride.

'I think we should go on that
spinny thing next,' said Wilbur, pointing
towards a fast-looking ride which
almost looked like a spider. There was
a car at the end of each arm and it
whizzed round and round like a very
fast roundabout.

'Umm . . . Pink Rabbit doesn't want
to try that ride, so I'm going to stay here
with him,' I said.

'Me too,' said Mum.

We walked over to the ride
and looked on as Mirabelle, Wilbur,
and Dad got into the little cars.
The ride started and we watched
them rise up into the air and start to
spin. Round and round they went,
with their hair flying out behind
them. Suddenly we saw a puff of
magic powder explode out of
Mirabelle's car, and all at once the
ride transformed itself into a
broomstick whirligig. Instead of cars,
my family were now sitting astride
broomsticks and spinning higher and
higher into the air. They weren't
even attached to the ride anymore.

I heard Mirabelle screech with delight, and the music from the ride started to blare across the fairground.

'Oh,' said Mum. 'I should have guessed she would do something!'

By the time the ride stopped, an even bigger crowd of people had gathered around.

'Wow!' they were saying. 'We want a go!'

The ticket seller was looking surprised but very pleased as he started to sell tickets to the next round of customers. Suddenly I didn't mind about the magic at all any more, even though it meant that the fair was not really a proper human one. It made me feel so happy that we had been able to help the fair people. My whole body tingled with excitement and pride. I wanted to do more! I pointed my wand at the roller coaster and shot a stream of sparks towards it. Fireworks began to shoot out of the

back of the carriage, as it sped along.
Rainbow glitter and sparkles fizzed
through the air.

'That's a nice touch, Isadora,' said
Mum. 'I think we're really making a
difference!'

'We are!' I said, feeling pleased.

'Where next?' asked Wilbur.

'The carousel!' I yelled.

'Good idea,' said Dad. 'We
had better get there before the
queues start!'

'I don't think there's much chance
of there being a queue,' said Mum, as we
made our way over to the carousel in the
middle of the fairground.

Sad and worn-looking horses
bobbed up and down on poles as the
carousel went slowly round and round,
playing a tune which kept getting stuck,
so that it played the same note over and
over again.

'Oh dear,' said Dad. 'This ride could
do with a bit of help.'

'I'll do it!' I said, jumping up and down excitedly. 'Let me try!'

I closed my eyes and waved my wand. When I opened them, the horses had transformed into big, sparkling unicorns and glittering dragons with scaly wings. The music became jaunty and cheerful.

'Oh wow!' said Mum. 'Well done, Isadora!'

'Beautiful!' said Dad.

We all raced towards the carousel. I chose a pink unicorn with a flowing mane and tail, and hopped on. Pink Rabbit sat proudly in front of me.

We started to go round and round.

But something was happening. The animals were starting to move. My unicorn began to stamp its feet and suddenly, with the pole still attached, it leapt right off the carousel and began to bob round the fairground.

Mum, Dad, Mirabelle, and Wilbur followed. We wound in and out of all the attractions, leaping through the air with tiny glowing stars streaming out behind us. People stared as we flew by, reaching for their phones, taking photos, and ringing their friends.

'Come to the fair!' they shouted. 'You won't believe your eyes!'

Eventually, the animals went back towards the carousel and hopped back on, waiting for the next round of people to get on.

'That was amazing,' said Mirabelle.

'It was my favourite!' I said.

There was a huge queue waiting
to get on the carousel now, and the
fairground was absolutely heaving with
people. I could see my friend Zoe climbing
onto the pink unicorn. I waved at her and
she waved back.

'I think we've done enough,' said
Mum. 'We should probably stop doing
magic now.'

'Yes,' agreed Dad. 'We don't want to
overdo it. Let's just enjoy ourselves now.
How about the ghost train?'

GHOST TRAIN

Entrance

'I love ghost trains,' said Mirabelle.

We queued up and as we stood there, I noticed a little glint in Mirabelle's eye. Once we were in the carriage, she started to rummage in her pocket for something.

'What are you doing?' I asked her, as the train lurched into life and we started to trundle along the little track, passing pretend monsters that leapt out of the shadows.

'Just one more thing,' said Mirabelle. 'The last thing, I promise.'

I saw her mix something up, and she threw it onto the monsters as we passed.

'It will just make the ride a little more interesting,' she explained.

But 'interesting' was not the word I would have used. When the train came out of the ride at the end, I could see people screaming and running away.

They looked *terrified*. Then I saw what
Mirabelle had done. The monsters, which
had been pretend before, had come alive,
and they were leaping out of the ghost
train and spilling out into the fairground,
chasing after the crowds!

Chapter FIVE

'Run!' screamed the people. 'Monsters!!'

'Oh Mirabelle!' wailed Dad, putting his head in his hands. 'What have you done?'

'Only the same as Isadora did to the carousel,' said Mirabelle defensively, but I noticed that she didn't seem quite so sure of herself now.

'Well you've gone too far!' said Dad. 'Look at all the people running away. All the good work we have done is ruined!'

We all watched as the monsters rampaged round the fair. They didn't seem dangerous to me, just excitable and curious. They had lost interest in the people and had spotted the bright lights of the food stands. Hungrily they began to gobble down hot dogs, popcorn, doughnuts, and every-flavoured candyfloss.

'Stop!' the owner of the food stall shouted. 'Help!' He looked dismayed.

'We have to stop them,' said Wilbur. 'We need to think of something!'

'I have an idea,' said Mum. She waved her wand and a leafy vine streamed out of it. She tied it into a lasso. Then she made six more.

'Take these,' she said, thrusting one out to each of us. 'Let's try and round the monsters up!'

We each grabbed a

lasso and ran away into the fair.

It was chaos. People were running all over the place and screaming, popcorn and hot dogs were flying through the air. I ran over to the food stall and threw my lasso, but the monsters saw me coming. They laughed, thinking it was a great game, and started to run away, scattering across the fair and starting to climb up the rides.

'Oh no!' cried Mum, 'I think we need a better plan.'

I flapped my little bat wings and rose up into the air. I tried to lasso another monster, who was crawling up the side of the rollercoaster, but it was too strong for me. I ended up being whooshed through the air as the monster took hold of my vine and started pulling me towards it. I needed something to fly on, something strong.

'The carousel!' I shouted, tugging the lasso away from the monster and flying over to my favourite ride. I landed on the back of a Pegasus, and tugged gently on the reigns. The magical creature leapt off the carousel and started to rise up into the air, flapping its big, beautiful wings. Its body felt strong and solid beneath me. Out of the corner of my eye I saw Wilbur jumping onto a dragon's back.

As we soared through the air, I spotted
Dad shooting towards the hall of mirrors
in a black bat-winged dodgem car, while
Mirabelle had leapt onto one of the
broomsticks from the whirligig. We
circled in the air above the fair. People
below stared up, open-mouthed.

I swirled my lasso in the sky and
brought it down gently round one of the
monsters who had jumped onto the roof
of the carousel.

It squeaked and looked surprised.

Mirabelle whirled her lasso and brought it down over a monster hiding behind the candyfloss stall. Wilbur caught two monsters who were busy climbing up the side of the roller coaster. It didn't take long to round them all up, and soon they were gathered into a little group in the middle of the fairground. Mum and Dad came running out of the hall of mirrors with one more monster, caught in the loop of their leafy vines.

'Fascinating place, that,' I heard Dad say. 'More mirrors than you can imagine!'

'It wasn't the best time to stop and do your hair though, was it?' said Mum, sounding slightly annoyed.

The monsters didn't look very scary at all—in fact, they looked a little bit frightened. I felt sorry for them.

'They won't hurt you!' I said to the crowd. 'They were just playing.'

'Though it was very naughty of you to eat all the food without paying,' said Dad, staring sternly at the monsters. 'You could make up for it by helping out at the fair!'

The monsters seemed excited by this idea.

'You could help sell the tickets and

popcorn,' I suggested. 'Look at all the crowds of people, the fair could probably do with some extra help.'

'We could!' agreed one of the ticket sellers. 'That would be wonderful!'

Chapter SIX

The monsters seemed pleased to be helping out. Enthusiastically, they bounded over to the different rides to help sell tickets. Some of them started picking up litter and putting it in bags. Some of them went back to the ghost train to add some extra excitement.

'This is great!' said the fair owner to Dad. 'You've really saved the day by rounding up all those monsters. We were worried we were going to lose all our new customers!'

'I don't think you're in danger of that now!' said Mum, looking around.

The fair was bursting with people. There were queues snaking away from every ride. Children were screaming and laughing with glee. The fairy lights were flashing, the music was blaring and suddenly I realized that the fair looked much more like the picture on my poster. I felt a glow of happiness flood through my whole body.

'You've really helped us out,'
continued the man. 'We are so
grateful.'

'Oh, it was nothing!' said
Dad, waving his hand dismissively
in the air.

'It was our pleasure,' smiled Mum. 'Though you do realize that most of this magic is temporary? The carousel animals and the monsters won't stay alive for ever, I'm afraid.'

'No worries!' said the man. 'We'll have made enough money tonight to do all the repairs we need to our rides, and more! The Funfair Spectacular will be spectacular once again!'

'Excellent!' said Dad.

'I'm so glad,' said Mum.

'We'd like to thank you all properly,' said the man, 'so please feel free to pick a prize of your choosing to take home.' He gestured towards a stall where there were lots of big cuddly toys.

'Ooh good,' said Dad, bounding over immediately and starting to examine the toys. I followed him and pointed to a big fluffy monster.

'Please can I have that one?' I asked.

'Of course!' said the fairground owner, hooking it down for me. Pink Rabbit bounced up and down beside me. I could tell he was getting a little bit jealous.

'Here's one for Pink Rabbit,' said Mum, handing him a tiny stuffed monster keyring. It was the perfect size for him and Pink Rabbit wiggled his ears in delight.

Just then, I noticed Zoe skip through the crowd towards me, with her mum in tow.

'Isadora!' she cried. 'Have you seen the carousel? It has unicorns on it!'

'I have!' I said. 'It's my favourite ride! Shall we go on it together?'

'I would love that!' said Zoe. She
took my hand and we made our way back
into the crowd, Pink Rabbit hopping
along beside me and my family following
close behind.

There was a long queue for the

carousel, but it didn't matter. We ate hot dogs and every-flavour candyfloss while we waited, and then Zoe and I hopped onto the unicorn together. Mirabelle and Wilbur sat on the dragon, bickering over who was going to sit at the front, and Mum and Dad chose a Pegasus pony with wings.

The music started, and we began to go round. Round and round we went. Our hair streaming out behind us in the breeze, and fairy lights flashing in our eyes. It didn't matter if we were at a human fair or a magical fair, I was just so happy to be there with my family and my friends, spinning and twirling

under the starry sky. Just like the
children on the poster for the Funfair
Spectacular.

Vampire-fairy cakes!

You will need an assistant so make
sure an adult helps you.

★ Preheat the oven to 180°C.

 ★ In a large mixing bowl, combine 100g
margarine with 90g caster sugar.

★ Mix in 2 eggs and 1 teaspoon
vanilla essence.

 ★ Sift in 100g self-raising flour
and 1 teaspoon baking powder.

★ Mix until all ingredients are combined,
then spoon a tablespoon of the mixture
into each of 12 muffin cases.

 ★ Before filling up each case, make a well in
the batter with a teaspoon or clean finger and fill
it with a teaspoon of strawberry jam.

★ Top off with another tablespoon of the cake mixture, then bake the cakes for 8-10 minutes. When they are golden brown, remove the cakes from the oven and cool on a wire rack.

★ Once cool, spread the top with a blob of strawberry jam. You can make fangs out of white, ready-rolled icing, use gummy sweets or even top with wearable plastic fangs.

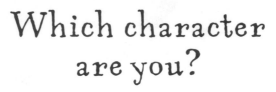

Which character are you?

Take the quiz to find out!

What is your favourite ride at the fair?

A. Rollercoaster with lots of loop the loops!

B. The carousel – my favourite is the unicorn

C. The helter skelter

What is your favourite food to eat at the fair?

A. A big bag of sweets

B. Candy floss

C. Hotdog

If you could do some magic at the fair, what would you do?

A. Make all the rides super-fast

B. I would transform the whole fair to make everything there totally magical!

C. I would conjure up a wizard hat helter skelter

Results

Mostly As

You are Mirabelle! You have a mischievous sense of fun and you are a brilliant friend to have around!

Mostly Bs

You are Isadora! You have an amazing imagination and you are a really generous friend.

Mostly Cs

You are Wilbur! You are cheeky and funny and you love to have fun.

Isadora Moon
Goes to School

Her mum is a fairy and her dad is a vampire
and she is a bit of both. She loves the night, bats,
and her black tutu, but she also loves the sunshine,
her magic wand, and Pink Rabbit.

When it's time for Isadora to start school
she's not sure where she belongs—fairy school
or vampire school?

Isadora Moon
Goes Camping

Half vampire, half fairy, totally unique!
Harriet Muncaster

Her mum is a fairy and her dad is a vampire
and she is a bit of both. So when they all go camping
at the seaside some things might happen that are not
quite normal . . .

From roasting marshmallows on a campfire to making
friends with a mermaid—special things happen when
Isadora's around!

Isadora Moon
Goes to the Ballet

Her mum is a fairy and her dad is a vampire
and she is a bit of both. Isadora loves ballet, especially
when she's wearing her black tutu, and she can't wait to
see a real show at the theatre with the rest of her class.

But when the curtain rises, where is Pink Rabbit?

Isadora Moon
Has a Birthday

ISADORA MOON

Has a Birthday

Half vampire, half fairy, totally unique!

Harriet Muncaster

Her mum is a fairy and her dad is a vampire
and she is a bit of both. Isadora loves going to human
birthday parties, and now she is going to have one of
her own!

But with her mum and dad organizing things, it's not
going to be like the parties she's been to before!

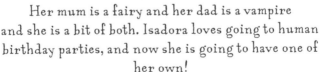

Isadora Moon
Goes on a School Trip

Her mum is a fairy and her dad is a vampire
and she is a bit of both. Isadora's classmates are all a bit
frightened when they go on a school trip to a spooky old
castle—what if they see a ghost?

It's up to Isadora to show her friends that sometimes
things that seem scary at first aren't scary at all!

Isadora Moon
Gets in Trouble

Isadora wants to take Pink Rabbit in to Bring
Your Pet to School Day, but her older cousin Mirabelle
has a much better plan—why not take a dragon?

What could possibly go wrong ...?

Harriet Muncaster

Harriet Muncaster, that's me! I'm the
author and illustrator of Isadora Moon.
Yes really! I love anything teeny tiny,
anything starry, and everything glittery.

Love Isadora Moon?
Why not try these too . . .